Anonymous

Historical Notes Respecting the Area and Political

Organization of the United States

Anonymous

Historical Notes Respecting the Area and Political Organization of the United States

ISBN/EAN: 9783337409777

Printed in Europe, USA, Canada, Australia, Japan

Cover: Foto ©Andreas Hilbeck / pixelio.de

More available books at **www.hansebooks.com**

HISTORICAL NOTES

RESPECTING

THE AREA AND POLITICAL ORGANIZATION

OF THE

UNITED STATES AND ITS GEOGRAPHICAL DIVISIONS,

WITH

THE STATISTICS

OF

AREAS, FAMILIES, AND DWELLINGS.

HISTORICAL NOTES RESPECTING THE ACQUISITION OF TERRITORY BY THE UNITED STATES; THE ERECTION OF EXISTING AND OBSOLETE POLITICAL DIVISIONS OF THE UNITED STATES, AND THEIR SUCCESSIVE CHANGES IN ORGANIZATION AND AREA.*

• ACQUISITION OF TERRITORY BY THE UNITED STATES.

CESSIONS BY STATES.—Prior to 1781, six only of the original thirteen States, viz: New Hampshire, Rhode Island, New Jersey, Pennsylvania, Maryland, and Delaware, had exactly defined boundaries . Of the remaining seven States, some claimed to extend to the Pacific Ocean and others to the Mississippi River. The States with inexact boundaries ceded their claims to lands west of their present limits in succession, as follows: March 1, 1781, New York. March 1, 1784, Virginia; the cession including the State of Kentucky and the parts of the States of Illinois, Ohio, and Indiana which lie south of the Forty-first parallel. Virginia reserved from this cession 150,000 acres of land. near the rapids of the River Ohio, and about 3,500,000 acres between the Rivers Scioto and Miami for military bounty lands. April 19, 1785, Massachusetts; including her claims to territory west of the present western boundary of the State of New York. September 14, 1786, Connecticut; the cession being the territory between the parallels of 41° and 40° 2′, and west of a north and south line drawn one hundred and twenty miles west of the present western boundary of the State of Pennsylvania. Connecticut then ceded all land and jurisdiction west of that territory, now situated in the State of Ohio, and yet known as "The Western Reserve of Connecticut." August 9, 1787, South Carolina; the territory ceded being a strip of land about twelve miles wide, south of the Thirty-fifth parallel and extending along the southern boundaries of the States of North Carolina and Tennessee to the Mississippi River. February 25, 1790, North Carolina; the cession constituting the State of Tennessee. This cession was accepted by Congress April 2, 1790. May 30, 1800, Connecticut; yielding all rights to territory and jurisdiction west of her present western boundary, and reserving the ownership of the soil of the Western Reserve, bounded as above recited. June 16, 1802, Georgia; receiving that part of the cession of South Carolina lying within her present limits, ceded all between her present western boundary and the Mississippi River, and between the South Carolina cession and the Thirty-first parallel. The foregoing cessions secured to the General Government all territory ceded by Great Britain, not included in the original thirteen States, as in the main now bounded. November 25, 1850, the State of Texas ceded all her claims to lands west of the Twenty-sixth meridian (103d Greenwich) and between 32° and 36° 30′ of latitude.

CESSIONS BY FOREIGN POWERS.—September 3, 1783, by Treaty with Great Britain the territory of the United States was declared to extend from the Atlantic Ocean westward to the Mississippi River, and from a line along the great lakes on the north, south ard to the Thirty-first parallel and the southern border of Georgia.

April 30, 1803, by Treaty with France the "Province of Louisiana" was ceded. Its western boundary as finally adjusted, February 22, 1819, by Treaty with Spain, ran up the Sabine River, to and along the Seventeenth meridian, (94th Greenwich,) to and along the Red River, to and along the Twenty-third meridian, (100th Greenwich,) to and along the Arkansas River, to and along the Rocky Mountains, to and along the Twenty-ninth meridian, (110th Greenwich,) to and along the Forty-second parallel to the Pacific Ocean. Its northern boundary has conformed to the boundary established between the British possessions and the United States. On the east it was bounded by the Mississippi River as far south as the Thirty-first parallel, where different boundaries were claimed. The United States construed the cession of France to include all the territory between the Thirty-first parallel and the Gulf of Mexico, and between the Rivers Mississippi and Perdido, the latter of which is now the western boundary of the State of Florida. Under this construction of the cession, the "Province of Louisiana" is now covered by those portions of the States of Alabama, D, and Mississippi, Ar, which lie south of the Thirty-first parallel; by the States of Louisiana, Arkansas, Missouri, Iowa, Nebraska, Oregon, Minnesota west of the Mississippi River, and Kansas, [except, Ak, the small portion thereof south of the Arkansas River and west of the Twenty-third meridian, (100th Greenwich;)] by the Territories of Dakota, Montana, Idaho, Washington, and that known as the Indian Country; and by the portion of the Territory of Colorado lying east of the Rocky Mountains and north of the Arkansas River, and all of the Territory of Wyoming north of the Forty-second parallel, and that portion of the Territory of Wyoming which is south of that parallel and east of the Rocky Mountains. In 1800, however, the "Province of Louisiana" had been ceded by Spain to France, Spain claiming that she ceded to France no

---

*The italic letters appearing throughout these Notes designate the parcels of territory which are described on pages 581 to 587, which are included in the table on pages 588 to 591, and are delineated on the map which faces page 571.

territory east of the Mississippi River except the "Island of New Orleans," and also contending that her province of West Florida included all of the territory south of the Thirty-first parallel and between the Perdido and Mississippi Rivers, except the "Island of New Orleans." Under this construction, the "Province of Louisiana" included on the east of the Mississippi River only that territory bounded on the north and east by the "Rivers Iberville and Amite and by the Lakes Maurepas and Pontchartrain."

February 22, 1819, Spain formally ceded the territory now covered by the State of Florida and by those portions of the States of Alabama, *D*, and Mississippi, *An*, which lie south of the Thirty-first parallel, and by that portion of Louisiana, *An*, which lies east of the Mississippi River and is not included in the "Island of New Orleans." This territory was styled by Spain the "Provinces of East and West Florida." Previous to this cession, by the authority of the Joint Resolution of January 15, 1811, and the Acts of January 15, 1811, and March 3, 1811, passed in secret session, and first published in 1818, the United States had taken possession of the East and West Floridas. By Treaty of January 12, 1828, between the United States and the United Mexican States, the boundary (see *ante*) of the "Province of Louisiana," which was established by treaty with Spain when Mexico was a part of the Spanish monarchy, was agreed upon as the boundary between the two republics.

December 29, 1845, Texas, formerly a portion of Mexico, and later an independent republic, was admitted to the Union.

February 2, 1848, Mexico ceded the territory now covered by the States of California and Nevada; also her claims to the territory covered by the present State of Texas, by the Territories of Utah, Arizona, and New Mexico, by portions of the Territories of Wyoming and Colorado, and by the unorganized territory west of the Indian Country, except that part of the Territory of Arizona, *Ck*, and that part of the Territory of New Mexico, *Cl*, lying south of the River Gila and west of the old boundary of New Mexico, which lands were ceded by Mexico December 30, 1853, and are known as the Gadsden Purchase.

By Treaty of March 30, 1867, exchange of ratification and transfer of title having been made June 20, 1867, Russia ceded Alaska. This cession made the line between the continent of Asia and America the northwestern boundary of the territory of the United States, and extended the territory of the United States northward to the Arctic Ocean. On the east this cession was bounded by a line beginning at the southernmost point of Prince of Wales Island (parallel of 54° 40') and running north along Portland Channel to the junction of the Fifty-sixth parallel of north latitude with the continent, and thence, along the summit of the mountains parallel to the coast, to and along the One hundred and forty-first meridian, to the Arctic Ocean. But where the crest of the mountains skirting the coast from the specified parallel to the meridian is more than ten marine leagues from the ocean, there the boundary is a line not more than ten marine leagues from the coast and parallel to its windings. This cession is separated from the main territory of the United States by the western part of the British possessions between the parallels of 51° 40' and 49° of north latitude.

THE POLITICAL DIVISIONS OF THE UNITED STATES.

THE ORIGINAL THIRTEEN STATES ratified the Constitution of the United States in succession, as follows: December 7, 1787, Delaware; December 12, 1787, Pennsylvania; December 18, 1787, New Jersey; January 2, 1788, Georgia; January 9, 1788, Connecticut; February 6, 1788, Massachusetts; April 28, 1788, Maryland; May 23, 1788, South Carolina; June 21, 1788, New Hampshire; June 26, 1788, Virginia; July 26, 1788, New York; November 21, 1789, North Carolina; May 29, 1790, Rhode Island.

The other States and the Territories were successively organized as political divisions of the United States as follows:

THE TERRITORY NORTHWEST OF THE RIVER OHIO.—By Ordinance of July 13, 1787, formed out of the cession from Virginia, being that part of the Territory south of the Forty-first parallel, and out of other territory acquired from Great Britain by the Treaty of 1783, being the part of the Territory north of the Forty-first parallel. Article V of this Ordinance provided that there should be formed from this territory not less than three nor more than five States; that three of the States should extend from the Ohio River northward; that the boundaries between these three States should be established as in the Ordinance described; and that Congress should have authority to form one or two other States out of that part of the Territory which lay north of an east and west line drawn through the southernmost extremity of Lake Michigan. The provisions of this article have been carried into effect by the erection, on the Ohio River, of the States of Ohio, Indiana, and Illinois, separated by the boundaries prescribed by the ordinance, and out of the land north of them of the States of Michigan, Wisconsin, and that part, Z, of the State of Minnesota which lies east of the Mississippi River.

THE TERRITORY SOUTH OF THE RIVER OHIO.—By Act of May 26, 1790, declared to be "one district" for the purpose of temporary government, and its government constituted like that of the Territory Northwest of the River Ohio, except as otherwise provided in the Act of April 2, 1790, accepting from North Carolina the cession of the State of Tennessee. The district included the territory comprehended in the present States of Kentucky a'nd Tennessee and the territory (T, A, and Cm) ceded to the United States by the State of South Carolina. It was limited on the south by the original State of Georgia, C, and by A s and B, which were ceded by the State of Ge orgia in 1802, and which by Act of March 27, 1804, became a part of Mississippi Territory.

THE DISTRICT OF COLUMBIA.—By Article 1, Section 8, of the Constitution of the United States, Co gress is empowered "to exercise exclusive legislation in all cases whatsoever over such district (not exceeding ten miles square,) as may, by cession of particular States and the acceptance of Congress, become the seat of government of the United States." The State of Maryland, by Act of December 23, 1788, ceded to Congress territo ry ten miles square for the seat of government of the United States. The State of Virginia, by Act of December 3, 1789, ceded territory ten miles square, or a less quantity, to the United States in Congress assembled, for the same purpose. By Act of July 16, 1790, amended March 3, 1791, these cessions were accepted, and made the permanent seat of government of the United States; and by the latter act the President was empowered to fix the boundaries within certain limits. By Proclamation of the President, March 30, 1791, a district ten miles square—from the State of Maryland, Co, sixty-four square miles, and from the State of Virginia, Cu, thirty-six square miles—was located and bounded. By Act of February 27, 1801, Congress assumed exclusive jurisdiction. By Act of July 9, 1846, the cession of Virginia (Cu) was retroceded.

VERMONT.—By Act of February 18, 1791, to take effect March 4, 1791, admitted as a State; formed from New York.

KENTUCKY.—By Act of February 4, 1791, to take effect June 1, 1792, admitted as a State; formed from Virginia.

TENNESSEE.—By Act of June 1, 1796, admitted as a State; territory ceded by North Carolina.

MISSISSIPPI TERRITORY.—By Act of April 7, 1798, formed subject to the claims of the State of Georgia to the jurisdiction and soil thereof, afterward ceded by the State of Georgia to the United States; bounded west by the Mississippi River, north by a line from the mouth of the Yazoo River due east to the Chattahoochee River, east by the Chattahoochee River, and south by the Thirty-first parallel. Consisted of C and At. From 1764 to 1783 these parcels were part of the British Province of West Florida, which included also all of the territory south of the 31st parallel and between the River Appalachicola on the east, and Lakes Pontchartrain and Maurepas and the River Mississippi on the west. By Treaty with Great Britain, in 1783, the portion of this Province north of the 31st parallel (C and At) was ceded to the United States, while the remainder was, by Treaty of the same year, ceded to Spain. These facts secured to the United States a title to the parcels in question (C and At) anterior to, and independent of, the cession by Georgia. By Act of March 27, 1804, there was added all that territory (A, B, As, and Cm) ceded by the States of Georgia and South Carolina, and lying between the Mississippi River and the State of Georgia, and between the territory as above bounded and the State of Tennessee. By Act of May 14, 1812, there was added the territory (D and Au) ceded by Spain, lying between the Pearl and Perdido Rivers. The whole Territory has since been absorbed by the States of Alabama and Mississippi.

INDIANA.—By Act of May 7, 1800, to take effect July 4, 1800, formed as a Territory from the Territory Northwest of the River Ohio. It consisted of all of the last-mentioned territory west of the present eastern boundary of the State of Indiana extended northward to the international boundary line, (Ab, Ae, Ad. Ae, Cg, W, X, Y, and Z.) By Act of April 30, 1802, that part (Ar, Bs) of the Territory Northwest of the River Ohio which was not included in the State of Ohio was annexed to the Territory of Indiana, which, by this increase, was extended eastward to include the whole of that now known as the lower peninsula of Michigan. By Act of March 26, 1804, to take effect October 1, 1804, (the act dividing the "Province of Louisiana," ceded by France, into the Territory of Orleans and the District of Louisiana,) the District of Louisiana, being all of the French cession west of the Mississippi River except the present State of Louisiana, (see cession by France, ante,) was committed to the government of the officers of the Territory of Indiana. By Act of April 19, 1816, the southern portion of the Territory of Indiana was enabled to become a State. By Joint Resolution of December 11, 1816, the same was admitted as a State.

OHIO.—By Act of June 30, 1802, formed as a State out of that part (Br) of the Territory Northwest of the River Ohio, which remained after the erection of the Territory of Indiana, by excluding all of that remainder lying north of a line drawn due east through the southernmost extremity of Lake Michigan. By the Act of June 15, 1836, (the enabling act for the State of Michigan,) and the Act of June 23, 1836, the northern boundary of the State was "established by and extended to" a direct line running from the southern extremity of Lake Michigan to the most northerly cape of Miami Bay, thence in Lake Erie to the international boundary line and to the Pennsylvania line. By this legislation *Ba* was added to the State.

LOUISIANA.—By Act of March 26, 1804, to take effect October 1, 1804, the southern part (*Am*) of the "Province of Louisiana," ceded by France, was constituted the Territory of Orleans, which, on the east of the Mississippi River, included only the land south of the "Rivers Iberville and Amite and the Lakes Maurepas and Pontchartrain." By Act of February 20, 1811, the same was enabled to become a State; by Act of April 8, 1812, to take effect April 30, 1812, the same was admitted as a State, with the name of Louisiana. By Act of April 14, 1812, there was added the territory (*An*) east of the Mississippi River and north of the "Rivers Iberville and Amite and Lakes Maurepas and Pontchartrain."

MISSOURI.—By Act of March 26, 1804, to take effect October 1, 1804, formed from the northern part of the "Province of Louisiana," and styled the District of Louisiana, but committed to the government of the officers of the Territory of Indiana. Its southern boundary was the present southern boundary of Arkansas, and it contained all the lands of the United States west of the Mississippi River not within the State of Louisiana. By Act of March 3, 1805, the same was organized as the Territory of Louisiana; by Act of June 4, 1812, to take effect on the first Monday of December, 1812, the same was reorganized as the Territory of Missouri. By Act of March 6, 1820, the northern part, *Ar*, of the Territory of Missouri, bounded as the present State of Missouri, except on the west, where it was limited by the meridian passing through the confluence of the Kansas and Missouri Rivers, was enabled to become a State under the name of Missouri. By Joint Resolution of March 2, 1821, admission of the same as a State further provided for; by Proclamation of August 10, 1821, admitted as a State. By Act of June 7, 1836, which took effect by the Proclamation of March 28, 1837, the western boundary of the State was extended to the Missouri River.

MICHIGAN.—By Act of January 11, 1805, to take effect June 30, 1805, formed as a Territory from the Territory of Indiana. It then consisted of *Ba, Ab, Ad*, and *Ar*, being mainly that known as the lower peninsula of Michigan, and bounded on the west and northwest by a line "through the middle of said lake [Michigan] northwardly to its northern extremity, and thence due north to the northern boundary of the United States, and on the south by a line drawn due east from the southern extremity of Lake Michigan." By Act of April 19, 1816, and Joint Resolution of December 11, 1816, *Ab* was taken into the State of Indiana. By Act of April 18, 1818, (the enabling act for the State of Illinois,) there was added to the Territory *Ae, Cy, X, Y*, and *Z*, being all that part of the former Territory of Indiana lying north of and not included in the State of Indiana, and that part of the Territory of Illinois which was not included in the State of Illinois. This addition extended the Territory westward to the Mississippi River. By Act of June 28, 1834, there was added to the Territory the territory (*Af, Ag, Ah, Ai*, and *N*) between the Mississippi River on the east and the Missouri and White Earth Rivers on the west, and between the northern boundaries of the States of Missouri and Illinois on the south and the international boundary line on the north. The Territory then extended from Lakes Huron and Erie westward to the Missouri River. By Act of June 15, 1836, enabled to become a State as now bounded; by Act of January 26, 1837, the same was admitted as a State. The remainder of the Territory of Michigan was afterward absorbed by the States of Wisconsin, Iowa, Minnesota, and a part (*N*) of the Territory of Dakota.

ILLINOIS.—By Act of February 3, 1809, to take effect March 1, 1809, formed as a Territory from the Territory of Indiana; was then bounded on the east by the present eastern boundary of the State of Illinois, extended northward to the international boundary line, on the north by British America, and on the west and southwest by the Mississippi River. By Act of April 18, 1818, enabled to become a State as now bounded; by Joint Resolution of December 3, 1818, the same was admitted as a State.

MISSISSIPPI.—By Act of March 1, 1817, formed from the western part of the final Territory of Mississippi and enabled to become a State; by Joint Resolution of December 10, 1817, admitted as a State.

ALABAMA.—By Act of March 2, 1817, formed as a Territory from the eastern part of the final Territory of Mississippi; by Act of March 2, 1819, enabled to become a State; by Joint Resolution of December 14, 1819, admitted as a State.

ARKANSAS.—By Act of March 2, 1819, formed as the Arkansaw Territory from the southern part of the Territory of Missouri; by Act of June 15, 1836, the same was admitted as the State of Arkansas.

MAINE.—By Act of March 3, 1820, to take effect March 15, 1820, admitted as a State; formed from Massachusetts.

FLORIDA.—By Act of March 30, 1822, made a Territory; by Act of March 3, 1845, admitted as a State; territory ceded by Spain.

THE INDIAN COUNTRY is a geographical but not an organized political division of the United States. By Act of June 30, 1834, regulating trade and intercourse with Indians, this Country was declared to be "all that part of the United States west of the Mississippi [River] and not within the States of Missouri and Louisiana and the Territory of Arkansas." This Act limited the Indian Country on the east by the present western boundaries of the States of Missouri and Arkansas, and north of these boundaries by the Mississippi River, on the west by the Pacific Ocean, and on the north and south by international boundaries. As the different tracts of land, which from time to time have been set apart, for the use of Indians, on the east side of the River Mississippi, have always been included within the boundaries of some political division, so this Indian Country on the west of this river was, when first bounded by the above-cited statute, identical in extent with the organized Territory of Missouri. The Country and the Territory have alike suffered successive losses of the same areas, and the Territory the loss of organization, until the government and the name of the Territory of Missouri have become obsolete, and the present Indian Country contains all of the land of the once Territory of Missouri which has not been absorbed by other political divisions. In 1850 the boundaries of the Indian Country were as follows: On the east, the present western boundaries of the States of Missouri and Arkansas; on the south, the Red River; on the west, the Twenty-third meridian (100th Greenwich) as far north as the Arkansas River, and along that river to the intersection of the Rocky Mountains and the Twenty-ninth meridian, (106th Greenwich,) and along that meridian northward to the proposed southern boundary of the original Territory of Nebraska, which became the northern limit of this Country. Within these limits, however, is included that part of the territory ceded by Texas to the United States which was not included in the Territory of New Mexico, being a parcel of land between the Arkansas River on the north and the present northernmost boundary of the State of Texas, and between the Twenty-third and Twenty-sixth meridians, (100th and 103d Greenwich.) Including this latter territory, the area of the Indian Country at 1850 was 195,274 square miles. By Act of May 30, 1854, the Territory of Kansas was erected, and its southern boundary, from the State of Missouri to the Twenty-third meridian, (100th Greenwich,) became the northern limit of the Indian Country. The limits of the Indian Country remain as they were left by that act; area, 68,991 square miles. A part of the territory above mentioned as ceded by the State of Texas was included in the Territory of Kansas. The residue, bounded on the north by the Territory of Colorado and the State of Kansas, on the east by the Indian Country, on the south by the State of Texas, and on the west by the Territory of New Mexico, and included between 36° 30' and 37° of latitude and the Twenty-third and Twenty-sixth meridians, (100th and 103d Greenwich,) having an estimated area of 10,800 square miles, still remains an unorganized portion of the public domain. In the construction of the subsequent Area table, for convenience, the area of this last-mentioned unorganized territory has been included in that of the Indian Country.

WISCONSIN.—By Act of April 20, 1836, to take effect July 3, 1836, formed as a Territory out of lands originally acquired by Treaty of Peace with Great Britain, in 1783, and other lands which were a part of the French cession. At the date of this act all these lands were in the Territory of Michigan. The part east of the Mississippi, (X, Z, and Cy,) had formerly been successively in the Territory Northwest of the River Ohio, and the Territories of Indiana, Illinois, and Michigan. The part of the Territory (Af, Ag, Ah, Ai, and X) west of the Mississippi River had formerly been in the Territory of Michigan. As so constituted the Territory of Wisconsin was bounded on the east, northeast, and on the south as far as the Mississippi River by the present boundaries of the State of Wisconsin; on the south, going westward from the Mississippi River, by the present northern boundary of the State of Missouri; on the west by the Missouri River, and on the north by the international boundary line. By Act of June 12, 1838, all of the Territory (Af, Ag, Ah, Ai, and X) west of the Mississippi River and of a line due north from the sources of that river to the international boundary line, was taken to form the Territory of Iowa. By Act of August 6, 1846, the Territory thus reduced in size was enabled to become a State, as now bounded; by Act of May 29, 1848, admitted as a State. The remainder of the Territory of Wisconsin not included in the Territory of Iowa or in the State of Wisconsin was, in 1849, included in the Territory of Minnesota.

IOWA.—By Act of June 12, 1838, to take effect July 3, 1838, formed as a Territory from the Territory of Wisconsin, and included all the territory (Af, Ag, Ah, Ai, and X) between the Mississippi and Missouri Rivers and north of the present northern boundary of the State of Missouri. By Act of March 3, 1845, admitted as a State, (Af and Ah,) having the same boundaries as at present, except that to the west the State extended only to the meridian of 17° 30', while on the north it extended to the parallel passing through the mouth of the Mankato or Blue Earth River. By Act of August 4, 1846, the State of Iowa was extended westward and restricted on the north to its present boundaries; by Act of December 28, 1846, re-admitted as so enlarged.

TEXAS.—By Joint Resolution of December 29, 1845, admitted as a State; had previously been an independent republic, and at an earlier date a portion of Mexico.

OREGON.—By Act of August 14, 1848, formed as a Territory out of the French cession, extending from the Forty-second parallel to the international boundary line, and from the Pacific Ocean eastward to the Rocky Mountains; area, 288,345 square miles. By Act of February 14, 1859, admitted as a State as now bounded; area, b
73

95,274 square miles. The part of the Territory not included in the State, 193,071 square miles, (*Bu*, *V*, *Ax*, *Bj*, and *Be*,) became the original Territory of Washington.

MINNESOTA.—By Act of March 3, 1849, formed as a Territory out of land east of the Mississippi River ceded by Great Britain, which was first in the Territory Northwest of the River Ohio, afterward successively in the Territories of Indiana, Illinois, Michigan, and Wisconsin, (*Z*,) and out of other lands west of the Mississippi River, ceded by France, which were successively in the Territories of Louisiana, (afterward organized as the Territory of Missouri,) Michigan, Wisconsin, and Iowa, (*N*, *Ai*, and *Ah*.) At the passage of this act, this Territory consisted of the parts of the Territories of Iowa and Wisconsin which were not respectively included in the States of the same names. As thus constituted the Territory extended from the northern boundary of the State of Iowa northward to the international boundary line, and from the western boundaries of the States of Wisconsin and Iowa to the Missouri and White Earth Rivers; area, 165,491 square miles. By Act of February 26, 1857, the portion of the Territory east of the present western boundary of the State (*Z*, *Ah*, and *Ai*) was enabled to become a State; by Act of May 11, 1858, the same was admitted as a State; area, 83,531 square miles. The part of the Territory not included in the State, 81,960 square miles (*N*) became a part of the Territory of Dakota.

CALIFORNIA.—By Act of September 9, 1850, admitted as a State; from territory ceded by Mexico.

UTAH.—By Act of September 9, 1850, formed as a Territory, extending from the Rocky Mountains westward to California, and from the southern boundary of the Territory of Oregon, being the Forty-second parallel, southward to the Thirty-seventh parallel; area, 220,196 square miles. By Act of February 28, 1861, 20,500 square miles, (*L*) set off to the Territory of Colorado. By Act of March 2, 1861, 10,740 square miles (*Bf*) set off to the Territory of Nebraska. By Act of March 2, 1861, 73,574 square miles (*Bg*) set off to the Territory of Nevada. By Act of May 5, 1866, 18,326 square miles (*Bh*) set off to the State of Nevada. By Act of July 25, 1868, 3,580 square miles (*Cd*) set off to the Territory of Wyoming. The remainder, 84,476 square miles, forms the present Territory of Utah.

NEW MEXICO.—By Act of September 9, 1850, which, by Proclamation of December 13, 1850, was declared to take effect at the date of proclamation, constituted a Territory; extending from California eastward to the Twenty-sixth meridian, and from the northern boundary line of Mexico northward to the Thirty-seventh parallel, while between the Rocky Mountains and the Twenty-sixth meridian it extended northward to the Thirty-eighth parallel; area, 213,807 square miles. By Act of August 4, 1854, the territory acquired from Mexico by the Gadsden treaty, 45,535 square miles (*Ck* and *Cl*) was annexed. It thus had a total area of 261,342 square miles, wholly constituted from cessions from Mexico and from the State of Texas. By Act of February 28, 1861, 14,000 square miles, (*I*) set off to the Territory of Colorado. By Act of February 24, 1863, 126,141 square miles (*E*, *Bi*, and *Ck*) set off as the Territory of Arizona, (see Arizona, *post*,) leaving 121,201 square miles, the present area of the Territory.

WASHINGTON.—By Act of March 2, 1853, formed as a Territory from the Territory of Oregon, and included all of the Territory not afterward included in the State of Oregon; area, 193,071 square miles, (*Bu*, *V*, *Ax*, *Bj*, and *Be*.) By Act of March 2, 1861, 4,638 square miles (*Be*) set off to the Territory of Nebraska. By Act of March 3, 1863, all of its territory then east of the Fortieth meridian and the Snake River, 118,439 square miles, set off to the Territory of Idaho, (see Idaho, *post*.) The remainder, 69,994 square miles, constitutes the present Territory of Washington.

KANSAS.—By Act of May 30, 1854, formed as a Territory, extending from the western boundary of Missouri westward to the Rocky Mountains, then the eastern boundary of the Territory of Utah; and from the Thirty-seventh northward to the Fortieth parallel, excepting that part of the Territory of New Mexico north of the Thirty-seventh parallel; area, 126,283 square miles, (*H*, *J*, *Aj*, and *Ak*.) By Act of January 29, 1861, that portion of the Territory east of the Twenty-fifth meridian, 81,318 square miles, (*Aj* and *Ak*) was admitted as a State. By Act of February 28, 1861, the remainder of the Territory, 44,965 square miles, (*H* and *J*,) was included in the Territory of Colorado.

NEBRASKA.—By Act of May 30, 1854, formed as a Territory from the public domain included between the western boundary (mainly the Missouri and White Earth Rivers) of the then Territory of Minnesota and the Rocky Mountains and between the Fortieth parallel and the international boundary line; area, 351,558 square miles, (*Ay*, *Az*, *Bc*, *Bd*, *K*, *O*, and *P*.) By Act of February 28, 1861, 16,035 square miles (*K*) set off to the Territory of Colorado. By Act of March 2, 1861, 228,907 square miles (*O*, *P*, *Ay*, and *Bd*) set off to the Territory of Dakota. Hitherto this area has been reported officially as 244,942 square miles through failure to deduct 16,035 square miles mentioned above, set off from the Territory of Nebraska to the Territory of Colorado in the month before the Territory of Dakota was organized. By the same act the Territory of Nebraska received from the original Territory of Washington 4,638 square miles, (*Be*,) and from the Territory of Utah 10,740 square miles, (*Bf*.) As thus constituted the Territory of Nebraska extended from the Missouri River westward to the Thirty-third meridian, and from the present northern boundary of the State of Nebraska, and west thereof from the Forty-third parallel southward to the present southern boundary of the State of Nebraska, and west thereof to the Forty-first parallel; its area was 121,994 square miles. By Act of March 3, 1863, there were set off to the Territory of Idaho 45,099 square miles, made up—1st, of 30,621 square miles (*Bc*) at first in the original Territory of Nebraska; 2d, of 4,638 square miles (*Bc*) once in the Territory of Oregon and afterward in the original Territory of Washington; and, 3d, of 10,740 square miles (*Bf*) originally in the Territory of Utah. These reductions left the area of the Territory of Nebraska 75,995 square miles. By Act of April 19, 1864, the same Territory enabled to become a State; by Act of February 9, 1867, admitted as a State.

COLORADO.—By Act of F e b r u a r y 28, 1861, formed as a Territory with an area of 104,500 square miles, consisting—1st, of 14,000 square miles (*I*) from the Territory of New Mexico; 2d, of 29,500 square miles (*L*) from the Territory of Utah; 3d, of 16,035 square miles (*K*) from the original Territory of Nebraska; and 4th, of 44,965 square miles (*H* and *J*) from the Territory of Kansas.

NEVADA.—By Act of M a r c h 2, 1861, formed as a Territory from a strip of the State of California and that part of the Territory of Utah west of the Thirty-eighth meridian. California, however, has not ceded the part of her territory included in the statutory boundaries of Nevada; area, exclusive of this portion of California, 73,574 square miles, (*Bg*.) By Act of March 21, 1864, enabled to become a State; October 31, 1864, proclaimed a State. By Act of May 5, 1866, there was added to the State of Nevada 18,326 square miles (*Bh*) from the Territory of Utah, and 12,225 square miles (*Bi*) from the Territory of Arizona. Present area of the State of Nevada, 104,125 square miles.

DAKOTA.—By Act of M a r c h 2, 1861, formed as a Territory, extending from the western boundaries of the States of Minnesota and Iowa westward to the Rocky Mountains, and from the present northern boundary of the State of Nebraska and to the west thereof from the Forty-third parallel northward to the international boundary line. It consisted of the portion of the original Territory of Nebraska north of the last-mentioned boundary, 228,907 square miles, (*O*, *P*, *Ag*, and *Bd*,) and of all of the Territory of Minnesota remaining after the erection of the State of Minnesota, 81,960 square miles, (*Nj*) having thus a total area of 310,867 square miles. By Act of March 3, 1863, the Territory of Dakota gave to the Territory of Idaho, of land at first in the original Territory of Nebraska, 161,935 sq. nare miles, (*Bd*, *P*, and *Ay*.) Hitherto this area has been officially reported as 177,970 square miles, erroneously including 16,035 square miles (*K*) which had passed from the original Territory of Nebraska to the Territory of Colorado before the organization of the Territory of Dakota. There then remained an area of 148,932 square miles. Hitherto this area has been officially reported as 150,932 square miles, which is the present area of the Territory of Dakota, the difference of 2,000 square miles (*P*) being accounted for by a strip of the present Territory of Dakota west of the Territory of Wyoming, which, at the period referred to, was not embraced in the Territory of Dakota. By Act of May 26, 1864, (the act erecting the Territory of Montana,) the Territory of Dakota received from the Territory of Idaho— 1st, land which had been first in the original Territory of Nebraska, next in the Territory of Dakota, afterward in the Territory of Idaho; in extent, 45,666 square miles, (*Bd* and *Pj*) 2d, land which had been at first in the original Territory of Nebraska, afterward in the Territory of Idaho; in extent, 30,624 square miles, (*Bc*:) 3d, land which had been originally in the Territory of Utah, next in the Territory of Nebraska, afterward in the Territory of Idaho; in extent, 10,740 square miles, (*Bfj*) 4th, land originally in the Territory of Oregon, next in the original Territory of Washington, next in the Territory of Nebraska, afterward in the Territory of Idaho; in extent, 4,638 square miles, (*Bc*.) Total received from the Territory of Idaho, 91,663 square miles. The area of the Territory of Dakota was thus 240,597 square miles. By Act of July 25, 1868, the Territory of Dakota gave to the Territory of Wyoming 89,665 square miles, being all of the above-mentioned 91,663 square miles, excepting 2,000 square miles (*P*) from the item 45,666 square miles. The present area of the Territory of Dakota (150,932 square miles) is thus obtained, but a tract containing 2,000 square miles (*P*) lies separated from the main body of the Territory by the entire extent east to west of the Territory of Wyoming. The present area of the Territory of Dakota is made up of *N*, *O*, and *P*.

ARIZONA.—By Act of F e b r u a r y 24, 1863, formed as a Territory (*E*, *Bl*, and *Ck*) from the western part of the Territory of New Mexico; area, 126,141 square miles. By Act of May 5, 1866, 12,225 square miles (*Bi*) set off to the State of Nevada. Present area, 113,916 square miles.

IDAHO.—By Act of M a r c h 3, 1863, formed as a Territory; then consisted of—1st, 118,430 square miles, (*V*, *Ax*, and *Bj*.) Hitherto this area has been officially reported as 123,077 square miles through failure to deduct 4,638 square miles (*Bc*) which, by Act of March 2, 1861, had been set off from the original Territory of Washington to the Territory of Nebraska. It was at first a part of the Territory of Oregon, and next in the original Territory of Washington, being what remained after the present Territory of Washington had been carved from it, less 4,638 square miles above mentioned; 2d, of 161,935 square miles (*Bd*, *P*, and *Ay*) once or the original Territory of Nebraska and subsequently in the Territory of Dakota; 3d, of 30,621 square miles (*Bc*) directly from the Territory of Nebraska;

4th, of 10,740 square miles (*Bf*) originally in the Territory of Utah, afterward in the Territory of Nebraska; 5th, of 4,638 square miles (*Be*) once in the Territory of Oregon, next of the original Territory of Washington, and afterward of the Territory of Nebraska; making the total original area of the Territory 326,373 square miles. By Act of May 26, 1864, the entire Territory of Montana, 143,776 square miles, (*Ax* and *Ay*,) was formed out of the Territory of Idaho. By the same act 91,663 square miles (see Dakota, *ante*) further were set off to the Territory of Dakota, leaving an area of 90,932 square miles. By Act of July 25, 1868, 4,638 square miles (*Bj*) once in the Territory of Oregon, next in the original Territory of Washington, and afterward in the Territory of Idaho, [not to be confounded with the 4,638 square miles (*Be*) twice mentioned just above,] were set off to the Territory of Wyoming. This transfer reduced the Territory to its present area, 86,294 square miles, all of which was once in the Territory of Oregon, and afterward in the original Territory of Washington.

WEST VIRGINIA.—By Act of December 31, 1862, declared to be a State, to be admitted at a date sixty days after proclamation to be made by the President. By Proclamation April 30, 1863, said act made to take effect J u n e 9, 1 8 6 3; from Virginia; area, 23,000 square miles.

MONTANA.—By Act of M a y 2 6, 1 8 6 4, formed as a Territory from the northeastern part of the Territory of Idaho. It consists—1st, of 116,269 square miles, *Ay*, at first part of the original Territory of Nebraska, next in the Territory of Dakota, and afterward in the Territory of Idaho; and, 2d, of 27,507 square miles, *Ax*, first in the Territory of Oregon, next in the original Territory of Washington, afterward in the Territory of Idaho. Aggregate area of the Territory, 143,776 square miles.

ALASKA.—By Treaty of M a y 2 8, 1 8 6 7, ceded by Russia. A geographical but not a political division of the United States. Area 577,390 square miles.

WYOMING.—By Act of J u l y 2 5, 1 8 6 8, formed as a Territory from portions of the then Territories of Utah, Dakota, and Idaho, aggregating 97,883 square miles, as follows: 1st, 30,621 square miles (*Be*) once in the original Territory of Nebraska, next in the Territory of Idaho, afterward in the Territory of Dakota; 2d, 10,740 square miles (*Bf*) originally in the Territory of Utah, next in the Territory of Nebraska, next in the Territory of Idaho, afterward in the Territory of Dakota; 3d, 4,638 square miles (*Bj*) once in the Territory of Oregon, next in the original Territory of Washington, next in the Territory of Idaho; 4th, 43,606 square miles (*Bd*) at first in the original Territory of Nebraska, next in the Territory of Dakota, next in the Territory of Idaho, afterward in the Territory of Dakota; 5th, 3,580 square miles (*Cd*) originally in the Territory of Utah; 6th, 4,638 square miles (*Be*) a tract the history and description of which are as follows: It is a right-angled triangle, having for its base the Forty-second parallel, its perpendicular the Thirty-third meridian, and its irregular hypothenuse the crest of the Rocky Mountains. It was at first the extreme southeastern projection of the original Territory of Oregon. It then occupied the same relative position in the original Territory of Washington, which extended westward to the Pacific Ocean. It next became a part of the western extremity of the Territory of Nebraska, which reached eastward to the Missouri River. It was next attached to Idaho, afterward to Dakota, from which it was set off to Wyoming; where it remains for the present. The Territory of Wyoming, therefore, consists of two parcels from each of the original Territories of Nebraska, Utah, and Oregon; and, while it has received no territory from Montana and Colorado, which adjoin it on the north and south, it nevertheless contains lands which have at different times been comprised in six other Territories, nearly one-half of the Territory having twice formed a part of Dakota.

DESCRIPTION OF PARCELS OF TERRITORY INTO WHICH THE TERRITORY OF THE UNITED STATES HAS BEEN DIVIDED BY THE SUCCESSIVE BOUNDARIES OF POLITICAL DIVISIONS.

ALABAMA, the State of: area, 50,722 square miles; is composed of *A, B, C,* and *D,* ceded by the States of Georgia and South Carolina, and by Spain.

A. Alabama, now in the State of: estimated area, 1,700 square miles. Being a strip of land twelve miles wide across the northern part of the State and adjoining the southern boundary of the State of Tennessee. Ceded by the State of South Carolina. Transfers: from the Territory South of the River Ohio to the Mississippi Territory and to the State of Alabama.

B. Alabama, now in the State of: estimated area, 27,722 square miles. Lying between the States of Georgia and Mississippi and between *A* and a line drawn due east from the mouth of the Yazoo River to the Chattahoochee River. Ceded by the State of Georgia. Transfers: from the Mississippi Territory to the State of Alabama.

C. Alabama, now in the State of: estimated area, 19,000 square miles. Between the States of Georgia and Mississippi and the southern boundary of *B* and the 31st parallel. Ceded by the State of Georgia. Transfers: from the Mississippi Territory to the State of Alabama.

D. Alabama, now in the State of: estimated area, 2,300 square miles. Between the Perdido River and the State of Mississippi and between the 31st parallel and the Gulf of Mexico. Ceded by Spain. Transfers: from the Mississippi Territory to the State of Alabama.

ALASKA, (the unorganized territory of:) area, 577,390 square miles. Ceded by Russia. (See page 574.)

ARIZONA, the Territory of: area, originally, 126,141 square miles. Consisted of *E* and *Bi; Ck* was added from Mexico and *Bi* was transferred to the State of Nevada; now consists of *E* and *Ck;* area, 113,916 square miles. Ceded by Mexico. Transfers: from the Territory of New Mexico to the Territory of Arizona.

E. Arizona, now in the Territory of: estimated area, 82,381 square miles. All of the Territory north of the River Gila. Ceded by Mexico in 1848. Transfers: from the Territory of New Mexico to the Territory of Arizona.

Ck. Arizona, now in the Territory of: estimated area 31,535 square miles. The part of the Territory south of the River Gila. Ceded by Mexico in 1853. Transfers: from the Territory of New Mexico to the Territory of Arizona.

ARKANSAS, the State of, or the Territory of, (the Territory obsolete:) area, 52,198 square miles. The State and the Territory identical in extent. Ceded by France. Transfers: from the District of Louisiana to the Territory of Louisiana, to the Arkansaw Territory.

CALIFORNIA, the State of: area, 188,981 square miles. Ceded by Mexico.

COLORADO, the Territory of: area, 104,500 square miles. Composed of *H, I, J, K,* and *L.* Ceded by France and Mexico.

H. Colorado, now in the Territory of: area, 4,000 square miles. Bounded on the north by the Arkansas River, east by the 25th meridian, south by the 37th parallel, and west by the 26th meridian. Ceded by Mexico; also by the State of Texas. Transfers: from the Territory of Kansas to the Territory of Colorado.

I. Colorado, now in the Territory of: area, 14,000 square miles. Bounded on the north and south by the 38th and 37th parallels, east by the 26th meridian, and west by the Rocky Mountains. Ceded, the part north of the Arkansas River, (if any,) by France; south of the river, by Mexico. Transfers: from the Territory of New Mexico to the Territory of Colorado.

J. Colorado, now in the Territory of: area, 40,965 square miles. Bounded north by the 40th parallel, east by the 25th meridian, south by the Arkansas River westward to the 26th meridian and by the 38th parallel, and on the west by the Rocky Mountains. Ceded from the original Territory of Kansas (being, with *H,* the portion of the Territory of Kansas which was not included in the State of Kansas) to the Territory of Colorado.

K. Colorado, now in the Territory of: area, 16,035 square miles. Bounded north and south by the 41st and 40th parallels, east by the 25th meridian, and west by the Rocky Mountains. Ceded by France. Transfers: from the original Territory of Nebraska to the Territory of Colorado.

L. Colorado, now in the Territory of: area, 29,500 square miles. Bounded north and south by the 41st and 37th parallels, east by the Rocky Mountains, and west by the 32d meridian. Ceded by Mexico. Transfers: from the Territory of Utah to the Territory of Colorado.

CONNECTICUT, the State of: area, 4,750 square miles. One of the original thirteen States.

DAKOTA, the Territory of: area, 150,932 square miles. At first it consisted of *N, O, P, Bd,* and *Ay:* area, 310,867 square miles; then *Bd, P,* and *Ay* were set off to the Territory of Idaho: area then, 148,932 square miles; next, *Bd, P, Bc, Bf,* and *Be* were received from the Territory of Idaho: area then, 240,597 square miles; next were transferred to the Territory of Wyoming all of the parcels last above mentioned, excepting *P.* The Territory of Dakota now consists of *N, O,* and *P.*

N. Dakota, now in the Territory of: area, 81,960 square miles. Bounded north by the 49th parallel, east by the western boundary of the States of Minnesota and Iowa, south by the Missouri River, and west by the Missouri and White Earth Rivers. Ceded by France. Transfers: from the "Province of Louisiana" and the District of Louisiana (afterward successively called the Territory of Louisiana and the Territory of Missouri) to the Territories of Michigan, Wisconsin, Iowa, Minnesota, and Dakota.*

O. Dakota, now in the Territory of: area, 66,972 square miles. Bounded north by the 49th parallel, east by the White Earth and Missouri Rivers, south by the present northern boundary of the State of Nebraska west of the mouth of Niobrara River, and west by the 27th meridian. Ceded by France. Transfers: from the original Territory of Nebraska to the Territory of Dakota.

P. Dakota, now in the Territory of: area, 2,000 square miles. Bounded north by the parallel of 44° 30', east by the 34th meridian, and south and west by the Rocky Mountains. Ceded by France. Transfers: from the original Territory of Nebraska to the Territory of Dakota, to the Territory of Idaho, to the Territory of Dakota.

DELAWARE, the State of: area, 2,120 square miles. One of the original thirteen States.

DISTRICT OF COLUMBIA, the: area, 64 square miles. Consisted of *Co* and *Cu*, 100 square miles. Ceded by the States of Maryland and Virginia; *Cu*, 36 square miles, was afterward receded to the State of Virginia.

FLORIDA, the State of, or the Territory of, (the Territory obsolete:) area, 59,268 square miles. Ceded by Spain as "East Florida."

GEORGIA, the State of: area, 58,000 square miles. One of the original thirteen States. Was composed of *U*, *B*, *C*, *Ax*, and *At*; now composed of *T* and *U*.

T. Georgia, now in the State of: estimated area, 1,500 square miles. Is a strip of land about twelve miles wide across the northern end of the State of Georgia, adjoining the States of North Carolina and Tennessee. Ceded by the State of South Carolina to the United States and received from the United States by the State of Georgia when the latter State made her cession to the United States. Transfers: from the Territory South of the River Ohio to the State of Georgia.

U. Georgia, now in the State of: estimated area, 56,500 square miles. Is the State except *T*, being the eastern part of the State as bounded when the State of Georgia ratified the Constitution of the United States.

IDAHO, the Territory of: area, 86,294 square miles. At first it consisted of *V*, *Bc*, *Bj*, *Ax*, *Ay*, *P*, *Bd*, *Be*, and *Bf*: area, 326,373 square miles; next, *Ay* and *Ax* were taken from it to form the Territory of Montana, and *Bd*, *P*, *Bc*, *Bf*, and *Be* were set off to the Territory of Dakota; area of the Territory then, 90,932 square miles; and, lastly, *Bj* was transferred to the Territory of Wyoming. The Territory now consists of *V*, ceded by France. Transfers: from the Territory of Oregon to the Territory of Washington, to the Territory of Idaho.

ILLINOIS, the Territory of, (obsolete:) estimated area, 144,662 square miles. Was composed of *W*, *X*, *Y*, and *Z*; ceded by Great Britain and the State of Virginia. Transfers: from the Territory Northwest of the River Ohio to the Territory of Indiana, to the Territory of Illinois. Absorbed by the States of Illinois and Wisconsin, the State of Minnesota east of the Mississippi River, and that portion of the State of Michigan west of the eastern boundary of the Territory.

ILLINOIS, the State of: area, 55,410 square miles. South of the 41st parallel ceded by the State of Virginia; north of the same, by Great Britain. Transfers: from the Territory of Illinois, *supra*.

INDIANA, the Territory of, (obsolete:) original estimated area, 205,151 square miles. Comprised *W*, *X*, *Y*, *Z*, *Ab*, *Ac*, *Ad*, *Ae*, and *Cy*; afterward *Ds* and *Ar* were added; estimated area then, 226,194 square miles. Ceded as was the Territory of Illinois, *supra*. Transfers: from the Territory Northwest of the River Ohio to the Territory of Indiana. Absorbed by the States of Indiana, Michigan, Illinois, Wisconsin, and that portion of Minnesota east of the Mississippi River, and by the parcel *Ds*, now in the State of Ohio.

INDIANA, the State of: area, 33,809 square miles. Composed of *Ab* and *Ac*. Ceded as was the Territory of Illinois, *supra*.

Ab. Indiana, now in the State of: estimated area, 1,200 square miles. Bounded on the south by a line drawn east from the southern extremity of Lake Michigan to the present eastern boundary of the State, and on the east by the present eastern boundary of the State; on the north by a line drawn due east and west ten miles north of the southern boundary of this parcel; on the west by a line from the southern point of Lake Michigan northward to its intersection with the northern boundary line of this parcel. Ceded by Great Britain. Transfers: from the Territory Northwest of the River Ohio successively to the Territories of Indiana and Michigan and to the State of Indiana.

Ac. Indiana, now in the State of: estimated area, 32,609 square miles. Being the State of Indiana, less *Ab*, with the same transfers as *Ab*, except that it was never in the Territory of Michigan.

---

* As all of the parcels of territory west of the Mississippi River which were ceded by France (save that part of the State of Louisiana lying west of the River Mississippi) were successively in the Province, the District, and the Territory of Louisiana, mention of these transfers will be omitted in subsequent descriptions of parcels.

INDIAN COUNTRY, the unorganized: area, 68,991 square miles. (See page 576.)

IOWA, the Territory of, (obsolete:) estimated area, 194,536 square miles. Consisted of *Af, Ag, Ah, Ai,* and *N.* Absorbed by the State of Iowa, by that part of the State of Minnesota lying west of the River Mississippi, and by the portion of the Territory of Dakota lying east of the River Missouri.

IOWA, the State of: area, 55,045 square miles. As first admitted consisted of *Af* and *Ah;* now consists of *Af* and *Ag.* Ceded by France.

Af. Iowa, now in the State of: estimated area, 36,720 square miles. Bounded north, east, and south by the present boundaries of the State, and on the west by the meridian of 17° 30'. Ceded by France. Transfers: from the Territory of Missouri successively to the Territories of Michigan, Wisconsin, Iowa, and to the State of Iowa.

Ag. Iowa, now in the State of: estimated area, 18,325 square miles. Bounded on the north and south by the present like boundaries of the State of Iowa, on the east by the meridian of 17° 30', and on the west by the Big Sioux and Missouri Rivers. Ceded by France. Transfers: the same as *Af.*

KANSAS, the Territory of, (obsolete:) area, 126,283 square miles. It consisted of *H, J, Aj,* and *Ak.* Ceded by France, except *H* and *Ak* and the part of *J* south of the Arkansas River, which was ceded by Mexico. The portion ceded by France was originally in the "Province of Louisiana;" the portion ceded by Mexico first appears in this Territory. Absorbed by the State of Kansas and a portion of the Territory of Colorado.

KANSAS, the State of: area, 81,318 square miles. Consists of *Aj* and *Ak.* Ceded, the part east of the 23d meridian and north of the Arkansas River, by France; the remainder by Mexico.

Aj. Kansas, now in the State of: estimated area, 73,542 square miles. Bounded north and east by the present boundary of the State of Kansas, on the south by the present boundary of the State of Kansas westward to the 23d meridian, then northward on that meridian to and along the Arkansas River, westward to the 25th meridian, which bounds this parcel on the west. Ceded by France. Transfers: from the Territory of Missouri successively to the Territory of Kansas and to the State of Kansas.

Ak. Kansas, now in the State of: estimated area, 7,776 square miles. Bounded on the north by the Arkansas River, east by the 23d meridian, south by the 37th parallel, and west by the 25th meridian. Ceded by Mexico. Transfers: from the Territory of Kansas to the State of Kansas.

KENTUCKY, the State of: area, 37,680 square miles. Ceded by the State of Virginia.

LOUISIANA, the Province of, (obsolete:) estimated area, 1,160,577 square miles. (See French Cession, page 573.)

LOUISIANA, the District of, (obsolete:) estimated area, 1,122,975 square miles. Consisted of the then Territory of the United States west of the Mississippi River not included in the State of Louisiana. (See Indiana, page 575.)

LOUISIANA, the Territory of, (obsolete.) Same area as the District of Louisiana: became the Territory of Missouri.

LOUISIANA, the State of: area, 41,346 square miles. It consists of *Am* and *An.* Ceded by France and Spain.

Am. Louisiana, now in the State of: estimated area, 37,602 square miles. Comprehends all of the State of Louisiana except the portion east of the Mississippi River and north of the "Rivers Iberville and Amite and Lakes Maurepas and Pontchartrain." Ceded by France. Transfers: from the Province of Louisiana to the Territory of Orleans, to the State of Louisiana.

An. Louisiana, now in the State of: estimated area, 3,744 square miles. Being the part of the present State of Louisiana not included in *Am.* Ceded by Spain.

MAINE, the State of: area, 35,000 square miles. Ceded by the State of Massachusetts. The portion of the State of Maine west of the River Kennebec and north of a right line connecting a point on that river one hundred and twenty miles from its mouth, with a point an equal distance from the mouth of the Piscataqua River, and in the general direction of that river projected northerly, appears never to have been within the old British Province of Main, or of Massachusetts Bay, or in the State of Massachusetts. If so, the title to this tract of land was vested directly in the United States by the Treaty of 1783, with Great Britain.

MARYLAND, the State of: area, 11,124 square miles. One of the original thirteen States. Originally, was *Ap* and *Co.* The District of Columbia, (*Co,*) 64 square miles, was ceded by the State of Maryland to the United States.

MASSACHUSETTS, the State of: area, 7,800 square miles. One of the original thirteen States, and then consisted of *Ao* and *Aq.* (See Maine.) After legislation granting and receiving sovereignty and jurisdiction by the States concerned, and after consent to the cession by Congress, the southwestern extremity of the State of Massachusetts known as the District of Boston Corner was, by the Proclamation of the Governor of the State of Massachusetts, dated January 11, 1855, declared ceded to the State of New York. Pursuant to an Act of the Legislature of Massachusetts, passed April 10, 1861, and to a Decree of the Supreme Court of the United States in the December term of 1861, the boundary between the States of Massachusetts and Rhode Island was so adjusted that these States interchanged parcels of territory. These two transactions transferred areas too small for further description, or for insertion in the succeeding table of parcels, or for delineation on the map of parcels.

MICHIGAN, the Territory of, (obsolete:) at first consisted of *Ab, Ad, Ar,* and *Bs;* estimated area, 41,243 square miles; next *Ae, Cg, X, Y,* and *Z* were added, and *Ab* was subtracted; estimated area then, 136,975 square miles; afterward *Af, Ag, Ah, Ai,* and *N* were added, increasing the area to 331,511 square miles. The Territory is now covered by the States of Michigan, Wisconsin, Iowa, Minnesota, by parts of the States of Ohio and Indiana, (*Bs* and *Ah,*) and by the part of the Territory of Dakota which lies east of the Missouri and White Earth Rivers.

MICHIGAN, the State of: area, 56,451 square miles. Consists of *Ad, Ae, Ar,* and *Y.* Ceded by Great Britain.

Ad. Michigan, now in the State of: estimated area, 19,000 square miles. Bounded on the south by a line drawn due east through a point ten miles north of the southern extremity of Lake Michigan to the eastern boundary of the State of Indiana, on the east by said boundary of Indiana extended northward until it intersects the western boundary of this piece of territory, which begins on the southern boundary of this parcel and runs northwardly through the middle of that lake to the point of intersection with its eastern boundary. Ceded by Great Britain. Transfers: from the Territory Northwest of the River Ohio successively to the Territories of Indiana and Michigan and to the State of Michigan.

Ar. Michigan, now in the State of: estimated area, 20,443 square miles. Being all of the State of Michigan east of the eastern boundary of the State of Indiana extended northward to the international boundary line. Same cession and transfers as *Ad.*

Ae. Michigan, now in the State of: estimated area, 7,180 square miles. Consists of all the territory (except *Cg*) bounded on the east by the western boundary of *Ar,* on the north by the international boundary line, on the west by the meridian of the eastern boundary of Illinois, on the south by the northern boundary of *Ab.* Same cession and transfers as *Ad.*

Y. Michigan, now in the State of: estimated area, 9,828 square miles. Bounded on the east by the western boundary of *Ae,* on the north and northwest by the international boundary line, on the south and southwest by the State of Wisconsin. Ceded by Great Britain. Transfers: from the Territory Northwest of the River Ohio successively to the Territories of Indiana, Illinois, and Michigan, and to the State of Michigan.

MINNESOTA, the Territory of, (obsolete:) area, 165,491 square miles. Consisted of *N, Z, Ai,* and *Ah.* Absorbed by the State of Minnesota and that portion of the Territory of Dakota lying east of the Missouri River.

MINNESOTA, the State of: area, 83,531 square miles. It consists of *Z, Ah,* and *Ai.* Ceded, east of the Mississippi River, by Great Britain; west, by France.

Z. Minnesota, now in the State of: estimated area, 26,000 square miles. Bounded on the north by the international boundary line, on the east by the boundaries of the State, on the west by the Mississippi River and a line drawn due north from its source to the international boundary line. Ceded by Great Britain. Transfers: from the Territory Northwest of the River Ohio successively to the Territories of Indiana, Illinois, Michigan, Wisconsin, and Minnesota, and to the State of Minnesota.

Ai. Minnesota, now in the State of: estimated area, 50,475 square miles. Bounded on the north by the international boundary line, on the east by a line drawn from the international boundary line due south to the source of the Mississippi River, and by the Mississippi River, southward to and along the northern boundary of *Ah,* to and southward along the meridian of 17° 30', to and westward along the parallel of 43° 30' to the western boundary of the State of Minnesota, and on the west by the western boundary of the State of Minnesota. Ceded by France. Transfers: from the Territory of Missouri successively to the Territories of Michigan, Wisconsin, Iowa, and Minnesota, and to the State of Minnesota.

Ah. Minnesota, now in the State of: estimated area, 7,056 square miles. Bounded on the north by the parallel passing through the confluence of the Blue Earth or Mankato and the Minnesota Rivers, on the east by the Mississippi River, on the south by the parallel of 43° 30', and on the west by the meridian of 17° 30'. Ceded by France. Transfers: from the Territory of Missouri to the Territories of Michigan, Wisconsin, and Iowa, to the State of Iowa, again to the Territory of Iowa, to the Territory of Minnesota, and to the State of Minnesota.

MISSISSIPPI TERRITORY, (obsolete:) at first consisted of *C* and *At;* estimated area, 33,056 square miles; afterward *A, E, As,* and *Cm* were added; estimated area, 91,978 square miles; afterward *D* and *An* were added; area, 97,878 square miles. The eastern part became the State of Alabama and the western the State of Mississippi.

MISSISSIPPI, the State of: area, 47,156 square miles. Consists of *As, At, An,* and *Cm.* Ceded by the States of South Carolina and Georgia, and by Spain.

Cm. Mississippi, now in the State of: estimated area, 1,700 square miles. A strip of land twelve miles wide across the northern part of the State of Mississippi, next the State of Tennessee. Ceded by the State of South Carolina. Transfers: from the Territory South of the River Ohio to Mississippi Territory and the State of Mississippi.

As. Mississippi, now in the State of: estimated area, 26,000 square miles. Lies south of *Cm* and north of *At.* Ceded by the State of Georgia. Transfers: from Mississippi Territory to the State of Mississippi.

At. Mississippi, now in the State of: estimated area, 14,956 square miles. South of *As*, and bounded on the north by a line drawn due east through the mouth of the Yazoo River and on the south by the 31st parallel. Ceded by the State of Georgia. Transfers: from Mississippi Territory to the State of Mississippi.

Au. Mississippi, now in the State of: estimated area, 3,600 square miles. All of the State of Mississippi south of the 31st parallel. Ceded by Spain. Transfers: from Mississippi Territory to the State of Mississippi.

MISSOURI. Territory of, (obsolete:) estimated area, 1,122,975 square miles. Was a reorganization of the Territory of Louisiana with the same boundaries. Consisted of all the "Province of Louisiana" except *Am*.

MISSOURI, the State of: area, 65,350 square miles. Consisted first of *Av*; afterward *Aw* was added.

Av. Missouri, now in the State of: estimated area, 62,182 square miles. Is the State of Missouri east of the meridian passing through the confluence of the Kansas and Missouri Rivers. Transfers: from the Province to the District and Territory of Louisiana, and to the Territory and State of Missouri. Was the original State of Missouri.

Aw. Missouri, now in the State of: estimated area, 3,168 square miles. Consists of all of the State west of *Av*. Transfers; same as *Av*, except that it was not in the original State of Missouri.

MONTANA, the Territory of: area, 143,776 square miles. Consists of *Ax* and *Ay*. Ceded by France.

Ax. Montana, now in the Territory of: area, 27,507 square miles. Bounded north by the 49th parallel, east by the Rocky Mountains to their junction with the Bitter Root Mountains, west by the Bitter Root Mountains to the 39th meridian, and on that meridian northward to the 49th parallel. Ceded by France. Transfers: from the Territory of Oregon to the original Territory of Washington, to the Territory of Idaho, to the Territory of Montana.

Ay. Montana, now in the Territory of: area, 116,269 square miles. Bounded north by the 49th parallel, east by the 27th meridian, south by the 45th parallel to the 34th meridian, southward on that meridian to the parallel of 44° 30′, westward on that parallel to the Rocky Mountains, and on the west by the Rocky Mountains. Ceded by France. Transfers: from the original Territory of Washington, and on the west by the Rocky Mountains.

NEBRASKA, the Territory of, (obsolete.) At first consisted of *Az*, *K*, *O*, *Be*, *Bd*, *P*, and *Ay*; area, 351,558 square miles; then *K* was set off to the Territory of Colorado; area then, 335,523 square miles; next, *O*, *P*, *Ay*, and *Bd* were set off to the Territory of Dakota, and at the same time *Be* was added from the Territory of Washington, *Bf* from the Territory of Utah; area then, 121,994 square miles; next, *Be*, *Bc*, and *Bf* were set off to the Territory of Idaho. The remainder of the Territory, area, 75,995 square miles, became the State of Nebraska.

NEBRASKA, the State of: area, 75,995 square miles. Ceded by France.

NEVADA, the Territory of, (obsolete:) area, 75,574 square miles. Consisted of *Bg*. Ceded by Mexico. Transfers: from the Territory of Utah to the Territory of Nevada.

NEVADA, the State of: area, 104,125 square miles. Consists of *Bg*, *Bh*, and *Bi*.

Bg. Nevada, now in the State of: area, 75,574 square miles. Bounded north and south by the 42d and 37th parallels, east by the 38th meridian, and west by a part of the eastern boundary of the State of California. Ceded by Mexico. Transfers: from the Territory of Utah to the Territory of Nevada, to the State of Nevada.

Bh. Nevada, now in the State of: area, 18,326 square miles. Bounded north and south by the 42d and 37th parallels respectively, east and west by the 37th and 38th meridians respectively. Ceded by Mexico. Transfers: from the Territory of Utah to the State of Nevada.

Bi. Nevada, now in the State of: area, 12,225 square miles. Bounded north by the 37th parallel, east by the 7th meridian, southeast by the Colorado River, and west by the boundary line of the State of California. Ceded by Mexico. Transfers: from the Territory of Arizona to the State of Nevada.

NEW HAMPSHIRE, the State of: area, 9,280 square miles. One of the original thirteen States. It seems that the portion of the State of New Hampshire which is north of the 45th parallel was not in the British Province of New Hampshire. If so, the title to this parcel was vested directly in the United States by the Treaty of 1783 with Great Britain.

NEW JERSEY, the State of: area, 8,320 square miles. One of the original thirteen States.

NEW MEXICO, the Territory of: area, 121,201 square miles. At first consisted of *Bm*, *Bi*, *E*, and *I*; area, 215,807 square miles; afterward were added *Ck* and *Cl*, part of the first cession from Mexico; area then, 261,342 square miles; first, *I* was set off to the Territory of Colorado; area then, 247,342 square miles; next, *E*, *Bi*, and *Ck* cut off to form the Territory of Arizona. Ceded by Mexico and by the State of Texas.

Bm. New Mexico, now in the Territory of: estimated area, 107,201 square miles. The Territory north of the Gila river and east of the western boundary of the former Mexican Territory of New Mexico. Ceded by Mexico in 1848.

Cl. New Mexico, now in the Territory of: area, 14,000 square miles. All of the Territory of New Mexico, except *m*. Ceded by Mexico in 1853.

NEW YORK, the State of: area, 47,000 square miles. One of the original thirteen States. Originally consisted of *Bn* and *Bo*. (See Massachusetts, *ante*.)

NORTH CAROLINA, the State of: area, 50,704 square miles. One of the original thirteen States. At first consisted of *Bp* and *Bq*.

OHIO, the Territory Northwest of the River, (obsolete:) estimated area, 265,558 square miles. Consisted of all the parcels west of the western boundary of the State of Pennsylvania, and between the Ohio and Mississippi Rivers, now covered by the States of Ohio, Indiana, Illinois, Michigan, and Wisconsin, and that part of Minnesota east of the Mississippi River and of a line drawn north from the source of the Mississippi River to the international boundary line. See the notes respecting each of the States included within the Territory.

OHIO, the Territory South of the River, (obsolete:) estimated area, 88,180 square miles. Consisted of the territory now covered by the States of Kentucky and Tennessee, and *Cm*, *A*, and *T*, now in the States of Mississippi, Alabama, and Georgia.

OHIO, the State of: area, 39,964 square miles. Formed as a State from the Territory Northwest of the River Ohio. Consisted of *Br*. Afterward *Bs* was added.

Br. Ohio, now in the State of: estimated area, 39,364 square miles. The portion of the State south of a line drawn due east through the southernmost extremity of Lake Michigan. Ceded north of the 41st parallel by Great Britain, south thereof by the State of Virginia. Transfers: from the Territory Northwest of the River Ohio to the State of Ohio.

Bs. Ohio, now in the State of: estimated area, 600 square miles. Bounded south by *Br*, and on the north by a line from the southernmost point of Lake Michigan to the northernmost point of Miami Bay. Ceded by Great Britain. Transfers: from the Territory Northwest of the River Ohio to the Territory of Michigan, to the State of Ohio.

OREGON, the Territory of, (obsolete:) area, 288,343 square miles. Originally composed of *Bt*, *Bu*, *V*, *Bj*, *Be*, and *Ax*, being all of the then Territory of the United States north of the 42d parallel and west of the Rocky Mountains; next, *Bu*, *V*, *Ax*, *Bj*, and *Be* were cut off to form the original Territory of Washington. The remainder of the Territory became the State of Oregon. Ceded by France to the United States. Transfers: from the Territory of Oregon to the State of Oregon.

OREGON, the State of: area, 95,274 square miles. Ceded by France. From the Territory to the State of Oregon.

ORLEANS, the Territory of, (obsolete:) estimated area, 37,602 square miles. Ceded by France. Transfers: from the "Province of Louisiana," and became the first State of Louisiana.

PENNSYLVANIA, the State of: area, 46,000 square miles. One of the original thirteen States. Was *Be*; afterward *Cp* was added.

Be. Pennsylvania, now in the State of: area, 45,684 square miles. All of the State south of the 42d parallel. Is the original State of Pennsylvania.

Cp. Pennsylvania, now in the State of. All north of the 42d parallel and west of the State of New York: area, 316 square miles. By the cession of the State of New York in 1781, and of the State of Massachusetts in 1785, the United States acquired title to this parcel of territory. By Resolution of Congress, passed June 6, 1788, the right of soil was conditionally sold to the State of Pennsylvania, and a survey of the parcel was ordered. By Resolution of September 4, 1788, the right of government and jurisdiction was relinquished to the State of Pennsylvania. By Treaty, made January 9, 1789, between the State of Pennsylvania and the Six Nations, the Indian title to this parcel was vested in the State of Pennsylvania. By Act of Congress, passed January 3, 1792, the President was authorized to issue letters-patent granting this parcel to the State of Pennsylvania. Such letters-patent were issued March 3, 1792.

RHODE ISLAND, the State of: area, 1,306 square miles. One of the original thirteen States. See Massachusetts.

SOUTH CAROLINA, the State of: area, 31,000 square miles. One of the original thirteen States. Previous to her ratification of the Constitution of the United States consisted of *Br*, *Cm*, *A*, and *T*.

TENNESSEE, the State of: area, 45,600 square miles. Formed from territory ceded by the State of North Carolina.

TEXAS, the State of: area, 274,356 square miles. Once a province of Mexico; achieved her independence from Mexico. Was admitted as a State, and ceded to the United States her lands west of the 27th meridian, now in the Territories of Colorado and New Mexico.

UNORGANIZED TERRITORY WEST OF THE INDIAN COUNTRY: estimated area, 10,800 square miles. Bounded by 36° 30' and 37° of latitude and the 23d and 26th meridians. Ceded by Mexico. (See Indian Country, page 576.)

UTAH, the Territory of: area, 84,476 square miles. Originally included *Bv*, *Bg*, *Bh*, *Cd*, *Bf*, and *L*; area, 220,196 square miles; first, *L* was set off to the Territory of Colorado; area then, 190,696 square miles; next, *Bf* was set off to the Territory of Nebraska, and *Bg* was set off to the Territory of Nevada: area then, 166,382 square miles; next, *Bh* was set off to the State of Nevada; area then, 88,056 square miles; next, *Cd* was set off to the Territory of Wyoming.

VERMONT, the State of: area, 10,212 square miles. From the State of New York. New Hampshire also claimed this Territory.

VIRGINIA, the State of: area, 38,348 square miles. One of the original thirteen States. Originally included *Ce*, *Cf*, and *Al*, and the portions of the States of Ohio, Indiana, and Illinois which lie south of the 41st parallel. First, ceded these last-named portions of existing States and also the State of Kentucky; next, ceded 36 square miles to become a part of the District of Columbia; this territory was afterward receded to the State; finally, the State of West Virginia was erected from her territory.

    Ce. Virginia, now in the State of: area, 38,312 square miles. Being the present State of Virginia, less *Ca*. Ceded by Great Britain. No transfers.

    Ca. Virginia, now in the State of: area, 36 square miles. That portion of the State of Virginia which was formerly a part of the District of Columbia. Ceded by Great Britain. Transfers: from the State of Virginia to the District of Columbia, and again to the State of Virginia.

WASHINGTON, the Territory of: area, 69,994 square miles. Originally included *Bu*, *V*, *Ax*, *Bj*, and *Bc*; area, 193,071 square miles; all parcels but *Bu* were taken into the Territory of Idaho. Ceded by France. Transfers: from the Province to the District, to the Territory of Louisiana, to the Territory of Missouri, to the Territory of Oregon, to the Territory of Washington.

WEST VIRGINIA, the State of: area, 23,000 square miles. Formed from the State of Virginia.

WISCONSIN, the Territory of, (obsolete:) area, 274,460 square miles. Originally included *X*, *Cy*, *Af*, *Ag*, *Ah*, *Ai*, *Z*, and *N*. All west of the Mississippi River was afterward included in the Territory of Iowa. The part east of the Mississippi River not included in the State of Wisconsin was afterward included in the Territory of Minnesota.

WISCONSIN, the State of: area, 53,924 square miles. Consists of *X* and *Cy*. Ceded by Great Britain to the United States.

    X. Wisconsin, now in the State of: estimated area, 53,424 square miles. All of the State, except that part on the east of the projected eastern boundary of the State of Illinois. Ceded by Great Britain to the United States. Transfers: from the Territory Northwest of the River Ohio successively to the Territories of Indiana, Illinois, Michigan, and Wisconsin, and to the State of Wisconsin.

    Cy. Wisconsin, now in the State of: estimated area, 500 square miles. Being that point of land between Green Bay and Lake Michigan which lies east of the eastern boundary of the State of Illinois extended northward. Ceded by Great Britain. Transfers: from the Territory Northwest of the River Ohio successively to the Territories of Indiana, Michigan, and Wisconsin, and to the State of Wisconsin. Unlike the rest of the State of Wisconsin, this parcel was never included in the Territory of Illinois.

WYOMING, the Territory of: area, 97,883 square miles. Consists of *Bc*, *Bd*, *Be*, *Bf*, *Bj*, and *Cd*.

    Bc. Wyoming, now in the Territory of: area, 30,624 square miles. Bounded north and south by the 43d and 41st parallels respectively, east by the 27th meridian, west by the Rocky Mountains. Ceded by France. Transfers: from the original Territory of Nebraska to the Territory of Idaho, to the Territory of Dakota, to the Territory of Wyoming.

    Bd. Wyoming, now in the Territory of: area, 43,666 square miles. Bounded north by the 45th parallel, east by the 27th meridian, south by the 43d parallel, and west by the Rocky Mountains, and at the northwest by the 34th meridian. Ceded by France. Transfers: from the Territory of Nebraska to the Territory of Dakota, to the Territory of Idaho, to the Territory of Dakota, to the Territory of Wyoming.

    Bc. Wyoming, now in the Territory of: area, 4,638 square miles. Bounded on the northeast by the Rocky Mountains, south by the 42d parallel, and west by the 33d meridian. Ceded by France. Transfers: from the original Territory of Oregon to the original Territory of Washington, to the Territory of Nebraska, to the Territory of Idaho, to the Territory of Dakota, to the Territory of Wyoming.

    Bf. Wyoming, now in the Territory of: area, 10,740 square miles. Bounded north and south by the 42d and 41st parallels, respectively, east by the Rocky Mountains, and west by the 33d meridian. Ceded by Mexico. Transfers: from the Territory of Utah to the Territory of Nebraska, to the Territory of Idaho, to the Territory of Dakota, to the Territory of Wyoming.

    Bj. Wyoming, now in the Territory of: area, 4,638 square miles. Bounded northeast by the Rocky Mountains, south by the 42d parallel, east and west by the 33d and 34th meridians respectively. Ceded by France. Transfers: from the original Territory of Oregon to the original Territory of Washington, to the Territory of Idaho, to the Territory of Wyoming.

    Cd. Wyoming, now in the Territory of: area, 3,580 square miles. Bounded north and south by the 42d and 41st parallels respectively, and east and west by the 33d and 34th meridians respectively. Ceded by Mexico. Transfers: from the Territory of Utah to the Territory of Wyoming.

Note.—The 6 foot-notes to the second page of this table, having the reference marks (¹) (²) (³) and (⁴) are on page 5 7.

		1780	1781	1784	1785	1787	1790	1791	1793
1	Alabama, the Territory of								
2	Alabama, the State of								
3	Alaska, the unorganized territory of								
4	Arizona, the Territory of								
5	Arkansaw Territory								
6	Arkansas, the State of								
7	California, the State of								
8	Colorado, the Territory of								
9	Connecticut, the State of	M (¹)	Id	Id	Id	Id	Id	Id	Id
10	Dakota, the Territory of								
11	Delaware, the State of	Q	Id	Id	Id	Id	Id	Id	Id
12	District of Columbia						Cn, Cn	Id	Id
13	Florida, the Territory of (§)								
14	Florida, the State of								
15	Georgia, the State of	U, B, C, As, At	Id	Id	Id	Id	Id	Id	Id
16	Idaho, the Territory of								
17	Illinois, the Territory of								
18	Illinois, the State of								
19	Indiana, the Territory of								
20	Indiana, the State of								
21	Indian Country								
22	Iowa, the Territory of								
23	Iowa, the State of								
24	Kansas, the Territory of								
25	Kansas, the State of								
26	Kentucky, the State of								Al
27	Louisiana, the Province of								
28	Louisiana, the District of								
29	Louisiana, the Territory of								
30	Louisiana, the State of								
31	Maine, the State of								
32	Maryland, the State of	Ap, Co	Id	Id	Id	Id	Ap	Id	Id
33	Massachusetts, the State of	As, Aq (¹)	Id	Id	As, Aq	Id	Id	Id	Id
34	Michigan, the Territory of								
35	Michigan, the State of								
36	Minnesota, the Territory of								
37	Minnesota, the State of								
38	Mississippi Territory								
39	Mississippi, the State of								
40	Missouri, the Territory of								
41	Missouri, the State of								
42	Montana, the Territory of								
43	Nebraska, the Territory of								
44	Nebraska, the State of								
45	Nevada, the Territory of								
46	Nevada, the State of								
47	New Hampshire, the State of	Bk	Id	Id	Id	Id	Id	Id	Id
48	New Jersey, the State of	Bl	Id	Id	Id	Id	Id	Id	Id
49	New Mexico, the Territory of								
50	New York, the State of	Bw, Bo (¹)	Bo, Bo	Id	Id	Id	Id	Bn	Id
51	North Carolina, the State of	Bp, Bq	Id	Id	Id	Id	Id	Id	Id
52	Ohio, the Territory Northwest of the River					W, X, Y, Z, Ab, Ac, Ad, Ac, Ar, Br, Bs, Cg.	Id	Id	Id
53	Ohio, the Territory South of the River						Bq, M, T, A Cm	Id	Bq, T, A, Cm
54	Ohio, the State of								
55	Oregon, the Territory of								
56	Oregon, the State of								
57	Orleans, the Territory of								
58	Pennsylvania, the State of	Bv	Id	Id	Id	Id	Id	Id	Bv, Cp
59	Rhode Island, the State of	Bw	Id	Id	Id	Id	Id	Id	Id
60	South Carolina, the State of	Bs, T, A, Cm	Id	Id	Id	Bx	Id	Id	Id
61	Tennessee, the State of								
62	Texas, the State of								
63	Unorganized ter. west of Indian Country								
64	Utah, the Territory of								
65	Vermont, the State of							Bo	Id
66	Virginia, the State of	Co, Cn, Cf, Al(§)	Id	Co, Cn, Cf, Al	Id	Id	Co, Cf, Al	Id	Co, Cf
67	Washington, the Territory of								
68	West Virginia, the State of								
69	Wisconsin, the Territory of								
70	Wisconsin, the State of								
71	Wyoming, the Territory of								

1796	1798	1800	1802	1803	1804	1805	1809	1812	1816	1817	
										A, B, C, D ...	1
											2
											3
											4
											5
											6
											7
											8
Id	Id	M	Id	Id	Id	Id	Id	Id	Id	Id	9
											10
Id	Id	Id	Id	Id	Id	Id	Id	Id	Id	Id	11
Id	Id	Id	Id	Id	Id	Id	Id	Id	Id	Id	12
											13
											14
Id	U, D, As	Id	T, U	Id	Id	Id	Id	Id	Id	Id	15
											16
							W, X, Y, Z	Id		Id	17
											18
		Ab, Ae, Ad, Ae, Cg, X, Y, Z, W.	Ab, Ae, Ad, Ae, Cg, X, Y, Z, W, Ar, Ds.	Id	Id (**)	Ae, Ae, Cg, X, Y, Z, W.	Ac, Ae, Cg.	Id	Ae, Cg.	Id	19
									Ab, Ae	Id	20
											21
											22
											23
											24
											25
Id	Id	Id	Id	Id	Id	Id	Id	Id	Id	Id	26
				(*)							27
					(*)						28
						(§)	Id				29
								Au, Au	Id	Id	30
											31
Id	Id	Id	Id	Id	Id	Id	Id	Id	Id	Id	32
Id	Id	Id	Id	Id	Id	Id	Id	Id	Id	Id	33
						Ad, Ab, Ar, Ds	Id	Id	Ad, Ar, Ds	Id	34
											35
											36
											37
	C, At	Id	Id	Id	C, At, Cm, As, A, D.	Id	Id	C, At, Cm, As, A, B, D, Au.	Id		38
										Cm, At, As, Au.	39
								(§)	Id	Id	40
											41
											42
											43
											44
											45
											46
Id	Id	Id	Id	Id	Id	Id	Id	Id	Id	Id	47
Id	Id	Id	Id	Id	Id	Id	Id	Id	Id	Id	48
											49
Id	Id	Id	Id	Id	Id	Id	Id	Id	Id	Id	50
Id	Id	Id	Id	Id	Id	Id	Id	Id	Id	Id	51
Id	Id	Dr, Ds, Ar									52
T, As, Cm	Id	Id	As, A, Cm, B (£)	Id							53
			Br	Id	Id	Id	Id	Id		Id	54
											55
											56
					Am	Id	Id				57
Id	Id	Id	Id	Id	Id	Id	Id	Id	Id	Id	58
Id	Id	Id	Id	Id	Id	Id	Id	Id	Id	Id	59
Id	Id	Id	Id	Id	Id	Id	Id	Id	I, £		60
Bq	Id	Id	Id	Id	Id	Id	Id	Id	Id		61
											62
											63
											64
Id	Id	Id	Id	Id	Id	Id	Id	Id	Id	Id	65
Id	Id	Id	Id	Id	Id	Id	Id	Id	Id	Id	66
											67
											68
											69
											70
											71

(§) The Spanish province of East Florida was S, now the State of Florida, and of West Florida was D, Au, and Au, respectively in the States of Ala., Miss., and La.

NOTE.—The foot-notes to the third and fourth pages of this table, having the reference marks (*) (†) (‡) (§) and (**) are on page 587.

#		1818	1819	1820	1821	1822	1834	1836	1837	1838	1845	1846
1	Alabama, the Territory of	Id										
2	Alabama, the State of			A,B,C,D	Id	Id	Id	Id	Id	Id	Id	Id
3	Alaska, the unorganised territory of											
4	Arizona, the Territory of											
5	Arkansaw Territory		F	Id	Id	Id						
6	Arkansas, the State of							F	Id	Id	Id	Id
7	California, the State of											
8	Colorado, the Territory of											
9	Connecticut, the State of	Id	Id	Id	Id	Id	Id	Id	dd	Id	Id	Id
10	Dakota, the Territory of											
11	Delaware, the State of	(')	Id		Id	Id	Id	Id	Id	Id	Id	Id
12	District of Columbia	Id	Id	Id	Id	Id	Id	Id	Id	Id	Id	Co
13	Florida, the Territory of					S	Id					
14	Florida, the State of										S	Id
15	Georgia, the State of	Id	Id	Id	Id	Id	Id	Id	Id	Id	Id	Id
16	Idaho, the Territory of											
17	Illinois, the Territory of											
18	Illinois, the State of	W	Id	Id	Id	Id	Id	Id	Id	Id	Id	Id
19	Indiana, the Territory of											
20	Indiana, the State of	Id	Id	Id	Id	Id	Id	Id	Id	Id	Id	Id
21	Indian Country						(*)	Id	Id	Id	Id	Id
22	Iowa, the Territory of									Af,Af,Ah, Ag,N	Ag,Af,Ah,N	Ah,Ai,N
23	Iowa, the State of										Af,Ah	Af,Ag
24	Kansas, the Territory of											
25	Kansas, the State of											
26	Kentucky, the State of	Id	Id	Id	Ik	Id	Id	Id	Id	Id	Id	Id
27	Louisiana, the Province of											
28	Louisiana, the District of											
29	Louisiana, the Territory of											
30	Louisiana, the State of	Id	Id	Id	Id	Id	Id	Id	Id	Id	Id	Id
31	Maine, the State of			Ao	Id	Id	Id	Id	Id	Id	Id	Id
32	Maryland, the State of	Id	Id	Id	Id	Id	Id	Id	Id	Id	Id	Id
33	Massachusetts, the State of	Id	Id	Aq	Id	Id	Id	Id	Id	Id	Id	Id
34	Michigan, the Territory of	Ad,Ar,Ts,Ae, Cg,X,Y,Z	Id	Id	Id	Id	Ad,Ar,Ds,Ae,Af, Ag,Ah,Ai,Cg, X,Y,Z,N	Ad, Ar, Ae, X, Y,				
35	Michigan, the State of							Ad,Ae,Ar, Y.	Id	Id	Id
36	Minnesota, the Territory of											
37	Minnesota, the State of											
38	Mississippi Territory											
39	Mississippi, the State of	Id	Id	Id	Id	Id	Id	Id	Id	Id	Id	Id
40	Missouri, the Territory of	Id	Id (I)	Id	Id (?)	Id	Id	Id	Id	Id	Id	Id
41	Missouri, the State of			Av.	Id	Id	Id	Av,Aw	Id	Id	Id	Id
42	Montana, the Territory of											
43	Nebraska, the Territory of											
44	Nebraska, the State of											
45	Nevada, the Territory of											
46	Nevada, the State of											
47	New Hampshire, the State of	Id	Id	Id	Id	Id	Id	Id	Id	Id	Id	Id
48	New Jersey, the State of	Id	Id	Id	Id	Id	Id	Id	Id	Id	Id	Id
49	New Mexico, the Territory of											
50	New York, the State of	Id	Id	Id	Id	Id	Id	Id	Id	Id	Id	Id
51	North Carolina, the State of	Id	Id	Id	Id	Id	Id	Id	Id	Id	Id	Id
52	Ohio, the Ter. Northwest of the River											
53	Ohio, the Territory South of the River											
54	Ohio, the State of	Id	Id	Id	Id	Id	Id	Br, Bs	Id	Id	Id	Id
55	Oregon, the Territory of											
56	Oregon, the State of											
57	Orleans, the Territory of											
58	Pennsylvania, the State of	Id	Id	Id	Id	Id	Id	Id	Id	Id	Id	Id
59	Rhode Island, the State of	Id	Id	Id	Id	Id	Id	Id	Id	Id	Id	Id
60	South Carolina, the State of	Id	Id	Id	Id	Id	Id	Id	Id	Id	Id	Id
61	Tennessee, the State of	Id	Id	Id	Id	Id	Id	Id	Id	Id	Id	Id
62	Texas, the State of										By,Cj,Ak, Il (‡)	Id
63	Unorganized ter. w. of Indian Co'try											
64	Utah, the Territory of											
65	Vermont, the State of	Id	Id	Id	Id	Id	Id	Id	Id	Id	Id	Id
66	Virginia, the State of	Id	Id	Id	Id	Id	Id	Id	Id	Id	Id	Co,Cf,Cn
67	Washington, the Territory of											
68	West Virginia, the State of											
69	Wisconsin, the Territory of						X, Z, Cg,Af, Ag,Ah,Ai, N.	Id	X, Z, Cg	Id	Id	
70	Wisconsin, the State of											
71	Wyoming, the Territory of											

(') Less F.   (‡) Less Av.   (‡) And part of Bm and of I, and of J south of the River Arkansas.

1848	1849	1850	1853	1854	1858	1859	1861	1863	1864	1866	1867	1868 (:)	
Id	Id	Id	Id	Id	Id	Id	Id	Id	Id	Id	Id	Id	1
											Ch	Id	2
												Id	3
							E, Bl, Ck	Id		E, Ck	Id	Id	4
													5
Id	Id	Id	Id	Id	Id	Id	Id	Id	Id	Id	Id	Id	6
		G	Id	Id	Id	Id	Id	Id	Id	Id	Id	Id	7
							H, I, J, K, L	Id	Id	Id	Id	Id	8
Id	Id	Id	Id	Id	Id	Id	O, P, A?, Bd, N.	Id	Id	Id	Id	Id	9
							O, P, A?, Bd, N.	O, N	O, N, Bd, P, Be, Bf, Be.	Id	Id	N, O, P	10
Id	Id	Id	Id	Id	Id	Id	Id	Id	Id	Id	Id	Id	11
Id	Id	Id	Id	Id	Id	Id	Id	Id	Id	Id	Id	Id	12
													13
Id	Id	Id	Id	Id	Id	Id	Id	Id	Id	Id	Id		14
Id	Id	Id	Id	Id	Id	Id	Id	Id	Id	Id	Id	Id	15
							V, Bj, A x, P, Ay, Bd, Be, Bf, Be.	V, Bj	Id	Id	V	16
													17
Id	Id	Id	Id	Id	Id	Id	Id	Id	Id	Id	Id	Id	18
													19
Id	Id	Id	Id	Id	Id	Id	Id	Id	Id	Id	Id	Id	20
Id	Id	Id	Id	Ci	Id	Id	Id	Id	Id	Id	Id	Id	21
Id													22
Id	Id	Id	Id	Id	Id	Id	Id	Id	Id	Id	Id	Id	23
				H, J, Ak, Aj	Id	Id							24
							Aj, Ak.	Id	Id	Id	Id	Id	25
Id	Id	Id	Id	Id	Id	Id	Id	Id	Id	Id	Id	Id	26
													27
													28
													29
Id	Id	Id	Id	Id	Id	Id	Id	Id	Id	Id	Id	Id	30
Id	Id	Id	Id	Id	Id	Id	Id	Id	Id	Id	Id	Id	31
Id	Id	Id	Id	Id	Id	Id	Id	Id	Id	Id	Id	Id	32
Id	Id	Id	Id	Id (ll)	Id	Id	Id (ll)	Id	Id	Id	Id	Id	33
													34
Id	Id	Id	Id	Id	N	Id	Id	Id	Id	Id	Id	Id	35
	N, Z, Al, Ab	Id	Id	Id	Id	Id							36
					Z, Al, Ah	Id	Id	Id	Id	Id	Id		37
													38
Id	Id	Id	Id	Id	Id	Id	Id	Id	Id	Id	Id	Id	39
(¶)	Id	Id	Id	(ll)			Id	Id	Id	Id	Id		40
Id	Id	Id	Id				Id	Id	Id	Ax, Ay	Id	Id	41
									Id	Id	Id	Id	42
				Ax, K, O, Be, Bd, P, Ay.	Id		Id	Ax, Be, Be, Bf.	Ax	Id		Id	43
											As	Id	44
							Dg	Id					45
Id	Id	Id	Id	Id	Id	Id	Id	Id	Bg	Dz, Bh, Di	Id	Id	46
Id	Id	Id	Id	Id	Id	Id	Id	Id	Id	Id	Id	Id	47
							Id	Id	Id	Id	Id	Id	48
			Bn, Bl, P, L	Id	Bn, Bl, E, I, Ck, Cl.	Id	Bn, Bi, E, Ck, Cl.	Bn, Cl	Id	Id	Id	Id	49
Id	Id	Id	Id	Id (ll)	Id	Id	Id	Id	Id	Id	Id	Id ...?	50
Id	Id	Id	Id	Id	Id	Id	Id	Id	Id	Id	Id	Id	51
													52
Id	Id	Id	Id	Id	Id	Id	Id	Id	Id	Id	Id	Id	53
Bt, Bu, Bj, Do, Ax, V.	Id	Id	Bt	Id	Id								54
						Bt	Id	Id		Id	Id	Id	55
Id	Id	Id	Id	Id	Id	Id	Id (ll)	Id	Id	Id	Id	Id	57
Id	Id	Id	Id	Id	Id	Id	Id	Id	Id	Id	Id	Id	58
Id	Id	Id	Id	Id	Id	Id	Id	Id	Id	Id	Id	Id	59
Id	Id	Id	Id	Id	Id	Id	Id	Id	Id	Id	Id	Id	60
Id	Id	By	Id	Id	Id	Id	Id	Id	Id	Id	Id	Id	61
Id	Id	Id	Id	Id	Id	Id	Id	Id	Id	Id	Id	Id	62
		Cj, H, Ak(**)	Id	Cj	Id	Id	Id	Id	Id	Id	Ba		63
		Bz, Bg, Bh, Cd, Bt, L.	Id	Id	Id	Id	Bz, Bh, Cd	Id	Id	Dz, Cd	Id	Ba	64
Id	Id	Id	Id	Id	Id	Id	Id	Id	Id	Id	Id	Id	65
Id	Id	Id	Id	Id	Id	Id	Id	Cv, Cu	Id	Id	Id	Id	66
			Bn, Bj, Bo, Ax, V.	Id	Id	Id	Da, V, Bj, Ax.	Bn	Id	Id	Id	Id	67
								Cf	Id	A l	Id	Id	68
													69
Z													70
X, Cg	Id	Id	Id	Id	Id	Id	Id	Id	Id	Id	Id	Bc, Bd, Be, Bf, Bj, Cd.	71

(ll) See Massachusetts, page 583. The transfer of 1855 is placed in column of 1854 to save space.   (::) No changes in organiza tion or area from 1868 to 1870.

NOTES TO THE PRECEDING TABLE OF PARCELS.

To the first and second pages of the table—

* And indefinitely westward.

† And the portions of *B₂, Ac*, and *W* lying south of the 41st meridian, and extended indefinitely westward.

‡ All of the then territory of the United States west of the River Mississippi, and that part of the State of Louisiana east of that river, and south of the "Rivers Iberville and Amite and Lakes Maurepas and Pontchartrain."

§ Same extent as the "Province of Louisiana" in 1803, less the portion of the Province within the boundaries of the present State of Louisiana.

¶ After the admission of the State of Tennessee, in 1796, these parcels were styled "the territory of the United States south of the State of Tennessee," until 1804, when they were added to Mississippi Territory.

‖ The Spanish Province of East Florida was *S*, now the State of Florida, and of West Florida was *D₁ Au*, and *Au*, respectively in the States of Alabama, Mississippi, and Louisiana.

** Also the District of Louisiana, being all of the French cession except the State of Louisiana, was committed to the government of the officers of the Territory of Indiana.

To the third and fourth pages of the table—

* Unorganized and identical in extent with the Territory of Missouri, being all the then territory of the United States west of the River Mississippi not within the present boundaries of the States of Louisiana, Missouri, and Arkansas. (See Indian Country, page 576.)

† Less *F.*

‡ Less *Ar.*

§ And part of *Bm* and of *I*, and of *J* south of the River Arkansas.

¶ All the territory of the French cession between the Rocky Mountains on the west and the River and State of Missouri on the east.

‖ Absorbed by the original Territory of Nebraska, the Territory of Kansas, and the Indian Country.

** Ceded by the State of Texas, and not included in the Territory of New Mexico.

†† See Massachusetts, page 553. The transfer of 1855 is placed in the column of 1851 to save space.

‡‡ No changes in organization or area from 1868 to 1870.

www.ingramcontent.com/pod-product-compliance
Lightning Source LLC
Chambersburg PA
CBHW020707260626
47157CB00008B/3180